Tiger, Tiger

by **Dee Lillegard**   illustrated by **Susan Guevara**

G. P. PUTNAM'S SONS   NEW YORK

For Brett. —D. L.

For those servants of the Muse who
create my Artist's Lifeline.
Thank you Dear Ashley, Dwight,
Julie, Martha and Mira.
Thank you Ricky.
Thank you Dearest Wilbur (forever)
and a starry mountain skyful of gratitude,
especially, to IGGY GIRL OF THE NORTH. —S. G.

Tiger! Tiger! burning bright
In the forests of the night,
What immortal hand or eye
Could frame thy fearful symmetry?

from THE TIGER *by William Blake*

One hot, hot day
    Pocu was playing
in his tiny village.

It was so hot, everyone
    wanted to take a nap.

"Go away, Pocu," they said.

Pocu grumbled angrily.
He slouched away,
and all the villagers
went to sleep.

As Pocu wandered alone,
he found a feather.

Swish. Pocu made the air cool.

Swish.
Pocu made the
flowers bloom.

Swish. Pocu made
a great murmuring shadow.

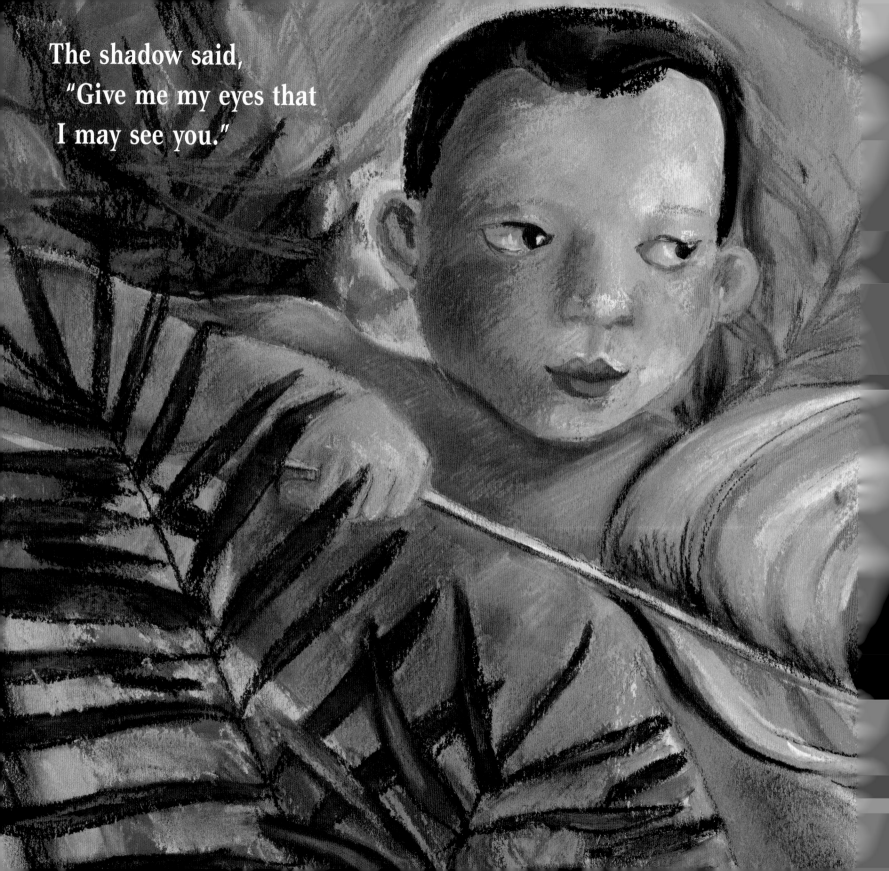

The shadow said,
"Give me my eyes that
I may see you."

Swish. Pocu gave the shadow
two bright eyes,
bright eyes burning in
a yellow-gold head.
And the shadow looked at him.

Pocu looked back.

Then the shadow said,
"Give me my paws that I may follow you."
Swish. Pocu gave the shadow
four big paws, four big paws on four sturdy legs.

Pocu walked on into the forest,
into the deep green forest.
And the shadow followed him.

Then the shadow said,
"Give me my body
that you may stroke me."
Swish. Pocu gave the shadow
a long, strong body—
a long, strong, yellow-gold body.
And slowly, carefully,
he reached out—and stroked it.

The shadow stretched and hunched and stretched again,
and followed Pocu through the bushes and the vines.

Then the shadow said,
"Give me my tail that I may stir the air."
Swish. Pocu gave the shadow
a fine, curling tail—
a fine, curling, yellow-gold tail.

The shadow stirred the air
and followed Pocu across the river
and a long, long way in the hot,
hot sun until at last the shadow said,

"Give me black stripes that
I may show you who I am."
Swish. Pocu gave the shadow
stripes of black,
jagged stripes of jetty black.

Then he whispered, "Tiger, Tiger . . ."

Tiger growled, "Lead me to your village
that I may be there in time for supper."

The monkeys screamed at Pocu.
The parrots screeched at him.
But Pocu led the tiger
back toward his village.

"I'm getting hungry,"
        Tiger growled.

"We will be there soon,"
        said Pocu.

He led the tiger through
        the bushes and vines,
the twisted, tangled bushes and vines.

Then *swish*.

Tiger yawned again.
He lay down upon
the mossy ground,
beneath the drooping
leaves and fronds.

"Sleep, Tiger," said Pocu.
And Tiger slept.

Then *swish*.
Pocu took back
Tiger's jagged black stripes.
He took back
Tiger's curling tail—
and his long, strong body.

Swish. Pocu took back
Tiger's four big paws—

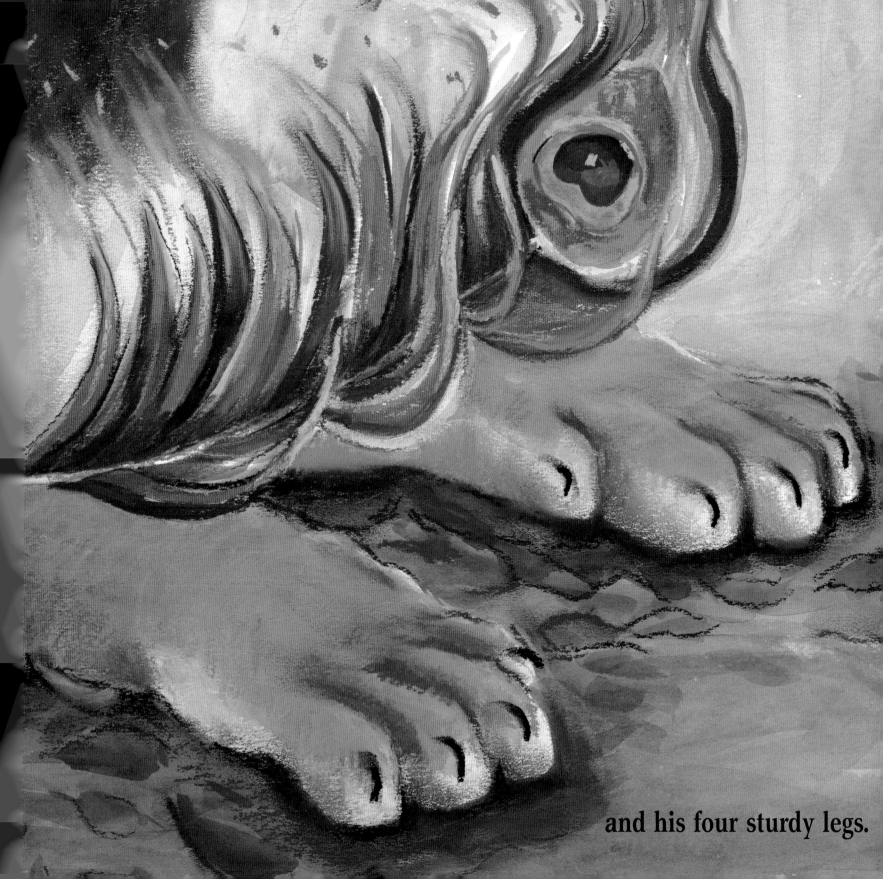

and his four sturdy legs.

He took back
    Tiger's two closed eyes,
the closed eyes that had burned bright
    in the yellow-gold head.

Then *swish*.

Pocu sighed.
He dropped the feather
and walked back into
his tiny village.

He was hungry,
very hungry.

And he was just in time for supper.